Lights!
Camera!

A Behind-the-Scenes Movie Guide

D1444707

Visit the Felicity Movie Headquarters Web site at **americangirl.com/movie**.

Questions or comments? Call 1-800-845-0005, visit our Web site at **americangirl.com**,
or write to Customer Service, American Girl, 8400 Fairway Place, Middleton, WI 53562-0497.

The Felicity movie is based on the Felicity stories by Valerie Tripp; telescript by Anna Sandor.

Photography by Brooke Palmer, Ben Mark Holzberg, Lori Woodley, Tamara England,
and Jodi Goldberg
Book illustrations by Dan Andreasen

Developed and written by Tamara England
Designed by Justin King
Produced by Jeannette Bailey, Mary Cudnohfsky, Julie Kimmell, Judith Lary, and Richmond Powers

Watch for Felicity's movie on The WB Television Network and on DVD—coming in November 2005.

Introduction

Felicity Merriman was created as a character in a series of books. Turning the Felicity books into a two-hour movie script was a challenge, one that required writing and rewriting, cutting and adding, and the reshaping of story elements. But the heart of Felicity's story remains the same on film as in the books—the story of a lively colonial girl growing up in Williamsburg, Virginia, when America was fighting to become an independent nation, when fierce loyalties divided families and friends, and when something as simple as a cup of tea was a hotly debated political issue that could separate best friends.

With the script in process, the cast selected, and the film location decided, hundreds of people came together in Toronto, Ontario, to prepare for and complete five intense weeks of filming. They made or rented costumes, wigs, and props; designed and built sets; hired extras—including horses; created special effects; ran lights, cameras, and sound equipment; prepared many hundreds of meals; and did whatever it took to bring Felicity's story to life on the screen. This book gives you a glimpse of what it was like behind the scenes of *Felicity: An American Girl Adventure*.

APPY *Felicity!* 1774 *Feli*

Felicity covers

American Girl designers
Heather, Stacey & Randy

Researching colonial gowns

Looking Like a Colonial Girl

Costume design started at American Girl, where Felicity was created as a book character and a doll. For book illustrations, accessories, and outfits for the Felicity and Elizabeth dolls, American Girl historians and costume designers researched clothing from colonial America and England in the 1770s. They found inspiration for costumes from paintings, patterns, books, and costume collections.

Felicity's looks and personality, like those of the other characters in her stories, also came from the books that first brought her to life.

American Girl™

American Girl™

SAVE

American Girl™

MEET *Felicity* 1774

IT BEGINS WITH A BOOK

MEET FELICITY

Felicity Merriman is a spunky, spritely ten-year-old girl growing up during the American Revolution. She is played by Shailene Woodley, a thirteen-year-old girl from California who has been acting since she was five years old.

MEET FELICITY'S FAMILY

Father — Felicity's father owns a general store in Williamsburg, the capital of the colony of Virginia. John Schneider, who has appeared in films, on the stage, and in many TV series, plays Father.

Mother — Felicity's mother takes care of her family with pride and love. Mother is played by Marcia Gay Harden, an award-winning actress who has worked on the stage, in films, and on TV.

Grandfather — Felicity's generous and loving grandfather, who understands what is important to Felicity, is played by Canadian actor David Gardner.

Nan — Felicity's six-year-old sister is sensible and sweet. Eulala Grace Scheel, the daughter of Marcia Gay Harden (Mother) is Nan. This is her first speaking role.

William — Felicity's quiet, almost-three-year-old brother likes mischief and mud puddles. Identical twins Kaden and Kolby Field took turns being William.

Penny — Penny is the independent and spirited horse Felicity loves. A quarter horse named Hilda, who has been in more than forty films, plays Penny in most scenes.

MEET FELICITY'S FRIENDS

Elizabeth Cole — Felicity's best friend is a quiet girl who is new to the colonies and who admires Felicity. Elizabeth is played by New Yorker Katie Henney.

Annabelle Cole — Elizabeth's snobby older sister, who thinks everything in England is better than in the colonies, is acted by British actor Juliet Holland-Rose.

Ben Davidson — An apprentice living with the Merrimans while learning to work in Father's store, Ben is played by Canadian Kevin Zegers.

Miss Manderly — Felicity's teacher is a gracious gentlewoman. Canadian actor Janine Theriault takes on the role of Miss Manderly.

Jiggy Nye — A cold-hearted scoundrel who mistreats his horses, Jiggy Nye is brought to vivid life by Canadian actor Geza Kovacs.

```
"FELICITY" - Anna Sandor - BLUE - 4/20/05          51.

Elizabeth fills Annabelle's cup and proffers milk and
sugar.

                      ELIZABETH
          Would you care for cake or a
          biscuit, Miss Cole?

                      ANNABELLE
                (taking a biscuit)
          Thank you, Miss Cole.

Elizabeth is coming around to Felicity.

                      ELIZABETH
          Tea, Miss Merriman?

Felicity looks at her, not knowing what to do...

                      ELIZABETH (CONT'D)
          Miss Merriman?

                      FELICITY
          Yes?

                      ELIZABETH
          Would you care for tea?

Felicity is in a panic of indecision. All eyes in the
room are on her.
Suddenly she remembers the very first lesson. She
swallows hard... Then gracefully turns her tea cup over,
places her spoon across it, and politely says...
```

Script revision of 4/20/05

Shaping the Script

Turning the six Felicity books into a telescript starts with a first draft, which may take weeks and even months. Rewrites, cuts, and additions continue during rehearsals and even into shooting.

Is this Felicity?!

Finding Felicity

Matching just the right actor to a role is called *casting*. The day that Felicity was found was a key day for the film!

Father's store,
from "Meet Felicity"

Showing a World

The Felicity book illustrations were a starting point for the Felicity film costume and set designers. But the special needs of designing for film meant big and small changes almost every step of the way.

GOING TO THE MOVIES

"FELICITY" – Anna Sandor – BLUE – 4/20/05

Elizabeth fills Annabelle's cup and proffers milk and sugar.

> ELIZABETH
> Would you care for cake or a biscuit, Miss Cole?

> ANNABELLE
> (taking a biscuit)
> Thank you, Miss Cole.

Elizabeth is coming around to Felicity.

> ELIZABETH
> Tea, Miss Merriman?

Felicity looks at her, not knowing what to do...

> ELIZABETH (CONT'D)
> Miss Merriman?

> FELICITY
> Yes?

> ELIZABETH
> Would you care for tea?

Felicity is in a panic of indecision. All eyes in the room are on her. Suddenly she remembers the very first lesson. She swallows hard... Then gracefully turns her tea cup over, places her spoon across it, and politely says...

> FELICITY
> Thank you, Miss Cole, I shall take no tea.

There is a moment of silence... Then...

> MISS MANDERLY
> Well done, Miss Merriman!

41   EXT. STREET – DAY   41   *

Felicity and Elizabeth are walking home. They pass a copper-colored HORSE pulling a carriage. Felicity stares at it longingly.

> ELIZABETH
> I suppose you are a Patriot now?

From script to screen: the moment when Felicity refuses tea at Miss Manderly's

The Script

In shaping the Felicity telescript, the scriptwriter started with the six Felicity books, but she had to make many adaptations. Some parts of the books were left out, while new scenes were added—scenes to take advantage of the visual nature of movie storytelling. Still other scenes were added for drama or as transition. Characters were changed slightly or left out completely. Finally, the order of some events changed to match the pacing and rhythm of the movie. And even after a script is finished, changes can occur when the movie is *edited*, or put together from beginning to end.

15

Shailene Woodley

John Schneider

Marcia Gay Harden

Katie Henney

Juliet Holland-Rose

Kevin Zegers

Eulala Grace Scheel

Janine Theriault

Geza Kovacs

Actor Peter Cockett looks just right as Elizabeth's and Annabelle's father.

Juliet, Shailene, and Katie during rehearsals—and before hair dyeing!

A real-life mother and daughter were cast as movie mother and daughter.

Auditions & Casting

To find the right actors for every role, auditions were held in New York, Los Angeles, and Toronto. Talent agents suggested actors, who were selected to perform scenes from the script while being videotaped. Because Felicity is the central character, deciding who would play her was the most important casting decision. After that, the other performers could be selected based in part on how they looked in relation to Felicity.

Kevin and Shailene as Ben and Felicity

Seeing Double

ACTING DOUBLE

Many actors beyond the main cast are involved in the movie. Some, such as Alanna Glass, work as "doubles," replacing principal actors in scenes where it is not noticeable. Child actors are limited to about five hours of work per day, so having an acting double allows filming to continue even if Shailene has to be off set.

Double touch-ups on the set

Alanna's hair is pinned up before she puts on her wig in the hair and makeup trailer.

RIDING DOUBLE

In addition to an acting double, an expert rider stood in for Shailene in some of the riding scenes—especially those featuring potentially dangerous stunts. Alyssa Smith Avery, who at thirteen is an accomplished rider, is the Felicity riding double.

STAND-IN

The final double, called a "stand-in," wears regular clothes but takes an actor's place when lighting is worked out between scenes. When the cameras are ready to roll, the actor will come back and step into the scene being filmed.

Alyssa, Hilda, and Shailene

A double has hair styling and costumes identical to those of the actor for whom she stands in.

A stunt double was hired to perform the dangerous stunts.

One of the Felicity film costume designers starting work on Felicity's lilac gown

Shailene in the completed lilac gown

Some of these elegant gowns and outfits were rented for the many extras hired for the Christmas Eve ball scene.

Designers inspired by a gown created for the Elizabeth doll selected this fabric to create a similar girl-sized gown for Katie.

Katie practices the minuet in her Christmas Eve ball gown.

Costumes

Movies in which old-fashioned costumes are an important part of the look are sometimes called "costume films." How the actors look and move comes in part from what they wear.

The Felicity film costume designers adapted many of the doll-sized costumes already created for the Felicity and Elizabeth dolls. They also turned to history for inspiration in creating additional gowns for Felicity and costumes for the many other actors in the cast. Using fabrics and patterns resembling clothing from the past, the costume design department cut and sewed dozens of gowns and outfits. Other costumes were rented for all or part of the film.

21

Sets & Locations

Recreating the look and feel of colonial Virginia is the job of the set designer. The set design team researched colonial architecture and decorating to recreate interiors and exteriors that look like Williamsburg in the 1770s.

Because there are no colonial-era buildings in Toronto, existing buildings were altered and others were temporarily constructed to achieve the special look and feel of colonial America. Turning the inside of a historical Toronto home into the Merriman home involved putting up removable wallpaper, constructing fake fireplaces, and renting 18th-century furniture and artifacts to fill the house. When filming is completed, everything will be returned to its original state.

A set being dressed, and then as seen during filming

Horse extras Pete and Marty with a wrangler

To film scenes in which Penny acts wild, Rick Parker, who owns many of the horses used in the film, is the stunt double for Jiggy Nye so that he can lead Penny through her stunts.

Felicity's beloved Penny was played by four different horses, but mainly by Hilda, an 18-year-old horse that has been in more than forty films.

24

Playing the Merrimans' horse Old Bess is a horse called Whitey.

Horses & Wranglers

More than a dozen horses appear in the Felicity film. The people who work with horses are called *wranglers*, and they play a crucial role in the making of the movie. Keeping horses calm, quiet, and safe in the commotion of filmmaking takes a special talent—especially when one of those horses is a mare with a four-day-old foal!

A stuffed horse was used to film the scene in which Penny gives birth to her foal, Patriot. The white blaze on the nose is being sprayed on!

Shailene learned to ride sidesaddle, bareback, and English with the help of wrangler Rick Parker.

Shailene and Amy review a complicated move prior to the filming of the Christmas Eve ball scene.

Learning the Minuet

In addition to learning lines, Shailene and other cast members learned to dance the minuet from dancer Amy Wright, who choreographed all the dance scenes. Rehearsals involved practicing the minuet—on tiptoe, please!—and a colonial jig called "Yellow Stockings."

Extras practice their steps before going inside, where the scene was filmed.

Shailene and Katie in a last-minute run-through before . . .

. . . their performance at the ball!

...ile Annabelle looks on, Miss Manderly ...inds Felicity that the minuet should be ...formed effortlessly and gracefully.

Practice makes perfect! Felicity and Elizabeth end their minuet at the Christmas Eve ball with graceful curtsies.

29

Cameras & Lights

Every scene is filmed by two cameras so that a scene can be shown from different angles. This creates more options when the movie is *edited*, or put together scene by scene. The director of photography, working with assistants and camera operators, decides how each camera will be positioned to best capture the scene.

Many types of cameras can be set up to film different situations. Some are even mounted on the backs of trucks. But no matter what type of camera is used, the actor's job is to act out his or her scenes as though the cameras weren't there.

Focus is measured very precisely from the camera lens to the actor, especially for complex takes like this one, where Shailene is being filmed in motion, as though riding a horse.

Huge "bounce" screens reflect the lights and sunlight to even out the lighting.

A "dolly camera" moves with the action by rolling on tracks.

Bright lights are used even outside in bright sunlight.

Monitors connected to both the cameras and the sound equipment allow producers and others to watch and listen to each "take," or filmed sequence.

This "boom" microphone has a wind screen covering it to shield the sensitive microphone from the noise of blowing wind.

The script supervisor makes note of everything that happens in each take so that continuity between shots is maintained.

Sound Recording

The sound of the slate clapping shut marks the beginning of each take. Because the camera's picture and the sound are recorded separately, the clap of the slate is used to *synchronize,* or bring together, the picture and sound. Most slates used today are digital and are linked to the computer that records the sound, but the actual sound of the clap can be a backup in case of problems with the digital time code embedded in the slate.

A boom microphone like this one is held above the actors on a boom pole and can record more than one actor's lines.

The slate here is held upside down for a "tail slate," which is used to mark the end of a take.

The director and Father

Jiggy Nye gets direction.

Working out a riding truck shot

In Production

Once the actual filming has started, a movie is considered to be "in production." Major rehearsals are complete, costumes and sets are made, and everyone focuses on how best to capture the story on film.

Many people take part in the production, but the director's job is one of the most important—before, during, and even after production is finished. The look and tone of the movie come from the many decisions the director makes early on, and from the people she picks to work with her. Once production starts, she directs the actors on how to move and deliver their lines and she consults constantly with the director of photography and other crew members to be sure the cameras and sound equipment are capturing her vision. Then, when everyone is ready and the cameras start to roll, the slate is clapped and the director calls out, "Action!"

Australian director Nadia Tass, shown her with John Schneider and Shailene, was als the director of the Samantha movie.

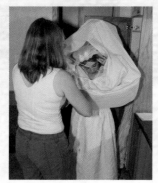

Dressing as Felicity

Dressing like a colonial girl requires patience—and help. After putting on a *shift*, a basic colonial undergarment, Shailene gets help from her mom and a dresser as she layers on a petticoat, then a gown stiffened with boning—much like the stays Felicity would have worn. While her bodice is laced behind her, Shailene pulls on stockings and slips into her shoes. Now she looks just like Felicity—except for the remote microphone clipped to her petticoat!

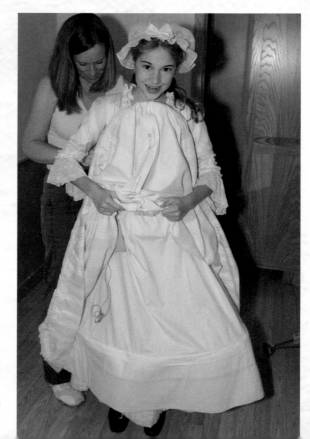

Kevin Zegers starting the day in the makeup chair

Wigs ready for extras

Makeup, Hair, Wigs

An actor's day starts in wardrobe, hair, and makeup. Hair and makeup artists keep careful records of each actor's makeup and "look" in order to match what was done in earlier scenes or to make changes for a new scene.

The wonderful world of wigs

Photographs taped to the mirror of Shailene's hair station help the stylist maintain consistency from day to day.

Shailene gets her hair fixed between takes. Hair stylists and makeup artists bring their supplies to the set for frequent touch-ups.

Extras

In addition to the main cast, dozens of Toronto actors were hired as *extras*, or background actors, for the Felicity movie. Extras work for just a day or two or for several days, until the scene or scenes requiring them have been completed. Just like the main cast, an extra's day starts in wardrobe, hair, and makeup. Then the extras wait—sometimes for a long time, sometimes not—for their scene or scenes to be run through and filmed.

These extras, dressed as Patriot soldiers prepared to fight the British, must be prepared to wait for their scene as well.

Extras are given specific directions about what to do when the cameras roll.

Grandfather walks with extras dressed as bounty hunters, complete with horses and a hound dog.

The use of extras brings depth and richness to crowd scenes.

Tanner Woodley, Shailene's younger brother, takes a bow as an extra.

An extra passes the time reading and making phone calls while waiting.

Waiting to be called

At School on Set

Imagine trying to get your schoolwork done while working. To ensure that all child actors complete the two to three hours per day of schooling that is required by law, a tutor or tutors are hired to work right on the set whenever there are children as part of the main cast. A trailer or other special area is turned into a schoolroom, and the young actors work closely with the tutors to complete the school assignments they bring from their teachers back home.

Tutors Laurel Branahan and Guido Janson are used to being flexible and having the actors come and go—sometimes in costume, sometimes not!

Felicity used a hornbook to practice her handwriting, but Shailene uses a laptop to complete her homework.

Tutors Laurel and Guido are on the set every day.

Laurel and Juliet work on lessons during rehearsals.

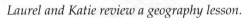
Laurel and Katie review a geography lesson.

Shailene fits in math review after dressing for the set.

On Set, Off Camera

Between scenes, while the cameras, lights, and sound equipment are made ready, actors have a chance to relax and get to know one another. There's always food nearby—although costumes have to be protected—and sharing magazines and stories helps pass the time. Everyone is there to work hard, but making friends is easy when sharing the intense experience of making a film together.

Shailene, Juliet, and Katie share a magazine between scenes.

Shailene relaxes on the set with her mother, Lori Woodley.

John Schneider, producer Lisa Gillan, and Shailene take a break at the snacks table on the set.

Alanna and Katie hang out together—and visit with Geza Kovacs and Shailene—during a lunch break.

Movie Magic

Movie magic happens in many ways. Turning summer into winter is the work of the special effects team. Techniques used to create the look of snow where there is none include laying down cotton batting and crushed ice, blowing artificial snow pellets into the air, and using computers to combine a snowy image with one that is not.

Other magic can happen through the use of stunts, the strategic placement of cameras, and the careful editing of film footage.

The green screen behind Felicity and Ben will be replaced by film of a snowy background, and the two pieces of film together will create one realistic image.

Where is there snow in June? On a movie set! With large roll of cotton batting, barrels full of crushed ice, and the hard wor of the special effects crew, a field of snow is created.

Shailene is filmed riding a fake "horse" mounted on a truck. This footage will be combined with other images and edited so that it looks like Shailene is riding Penny.

For this carefully planned stunt, skillful editing will combine the film footage of Shailene riding Penny with a stunt double's jump and fall off the horse.

Movie magic also allows two young actors to be transformed from modern girls in the year 2005 to colonial girls in 1775.

Through the combination of story and script, costumes and cameras, special effects and acting, the magic of the movies can take us all to another time and place.